# Pirates Ahoy!

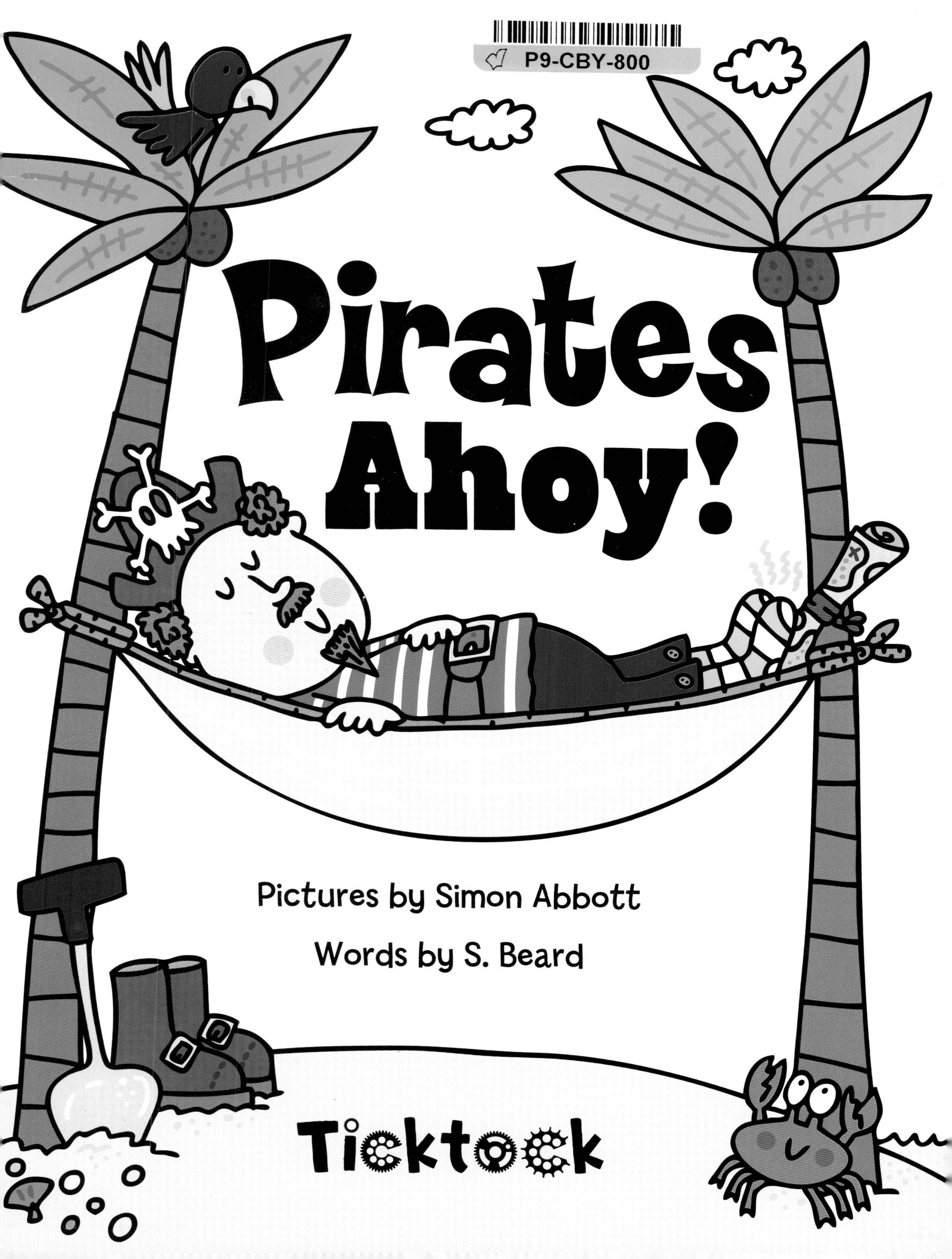



Pictures by Simon Abbott

Words by S. Beard

Ticktock

# Scary Seas

Pirates were fierce robbers who sailed the seas. The most famous pirates lived around 300 years ago, stealing from other ships and lands. Let's see where they got up to no good.

Ships in the **Caribbean Sea** were laden with riches (sugar, money, and slaves), and the many islands were perfect hiding places - making this the ideal place for piracy!

The Spanish ruled the Atlantic around **Central and South America**. Their ships were loaded with silver and headed for Spain - perfect for looting.

Many pirates were from **Great Britain**, but they also came from China, America, and Spain - to name just a few.

Some pirates were actually top sailors allowed by a king or queen to go and rob their enemies. They were known as "**privateers**."

EUROPE
ASIA
AFRICA
AUSTRALIA
Pirates from North America would raid ships in the **Indian Ocean** for fancy clothing and fabrics.
**Madagascar** was a pirate's playground. Pirates stopped off here to enjoy their loot and unwind.
The sea off the West African coast was a good place to raid ships carrying **gold** and **ivory** - elephants' tusks.
**Captain Kidd** was a privateer sent out by the king.
In his time, pirate captain **Black Bart** captured more than 470 vessels!
This makes 471, boss!
WOW!

# All Aboard!

Pirates' ships looked fantastic and often quite scary. They were smelly and crowded, but they were home.

**Flag**

When they were trying to frighten other ships, pirates flew scary flags.

**Ratlines**

The ropes that looked like ladders were called ratlines. These were for climbing up the masts and getting to the sails quickly.

Last one to the top's a wimp!
Welcome aboard, landlubber!

**Captain's Quarters**

The captain had his own room, which could be quite fancy.

**Hand Pump**

A hand pump was useful for getting water out of the ship.

**Bilge**

Water collected in the bilge, at the bottom of the ship. It was teeming with dead and living bugs and rats, and it stunk. Yuck.

### Did You Know?

Pirates didn't have a toilet and used the "**head**" instead - a board with a hole in it, which they put over the side!

Every ship needed **gunpowder** but it was dangerous stuff. Crew members were always scared of blowing up the ship by accident whenever they lit a match.

**Deck**

The upper decks had to be reinforced with extra wood to hold the weight of cannons - or guns as they were always called.

**Quarters**

Everyone slept together in hammocks in quarters called the forecastle (say foke-sul). It was smelly and cramped.

**Stores**

Food and water (both a bit nasty) were kept in the stores.

# Meet the Crew

Pirates were an odd bunch - poor sailors and fishermen, escaped slaves, and those who were just plain greedy. Once on board, they all knew what they had to do.

**The Quartermaster** was the ship's judge and general supervisor. He divided out the loot.

**The Sailing Master** guided the ship and decided which way it would go.

**The Captain** Many pirate crews actually chose their own captain by voting for him.

**The Surgeon** put wounded pirates back together again or chopped broken bits off.

Pirate captain **Black Bart** would never attack on a Sunday.

Every pirate ship had its own rules of behavio such as "**No Stealing**" (from a fellow pirate!).

What about me!
The Boatswain
was in charge of the sails and the rigging.
The Riggers
were the ones who climbed up the masts to roll up or unfurl the sails. It was an extradangerous job.
The Master Gunner was in charge of the guns.
The Carpenter
kept the ship in one piece.
The Cooper
made and kept the barrels - which held the water and food.
And the rest were just pirates - or "gentlemen of fortune," as they liked to be called.
Black Bart's crew insisted it be allowed to use his cutlery and plates. Or else!
Every crew needed entertaining and would always be on the lookout for musicians to recruit!
WOW!

# Pirate Chores

A pirate crew had lots of tough jobs to do. Some of these were quite dangerous.

Let's rock! Aaaargh!
I thought I was going on a cruise!

The decks had to be **mopped** with vinegar to keep them clean.

**Sails** had to b
pulled to the prope
positions to keep th
ship's speed up
Exhausting

If it was mealtime, the men in the band had to **play music.**

Every now and then, when the ship
was moored at low tide, the crew
had to scrape the barnacles off
it and mend and seal any holes wit
tar. This was called **careening.**
Sticky, stinky hard work.

Working in the **rigging** - the ropes that hold and control the sails - was dangerous but had to be done. Being barefoot helped the men grip the ropes as they climbed.

Sails often needed **mending**. The boatswain set men to work stitching up holes and tears.

To keep the **guns** working, they had to be cleaned.

**Did You Know?**
If the ship was in such a heavy storm that it was in real danger of sinking, the crew might have to chop down the masts to steady it.

One really dangerous job was taking gunpowder to the guns in a battle. The boys who did this were called **Powder Monkeys**.

# Pirate Style

Pirate captains loved to dress up in the fanciest clothes they'd taken from their victims. Everyone else dressed a bit more sensibly for life at sea.

Pirates had **beards** because they couldn't shave very often. They used a thread to tie their long hair or beards up so they didn't get caught in the ropes.

**Belts** were made from lengths of old rope.

Baggy **woollen pants** were cut off at the knees to stop the bottoms from getting too wet.

A stolen fancy **hat** showed that the captain was in charge. Other pirates might have worn headscarves or knitted caps.

Wearing fancy, frilly **jackets** and **shirts** made the pirates look important. A really lucky pirate would have had a canvas jacket or coat to wear in cold weather.

**Cutlass.** While some pirates might have had pistols, too, these short swords were very useful - for chores and for fighting.

Captains may have worn **shoes**, but most pirates went barefoot.

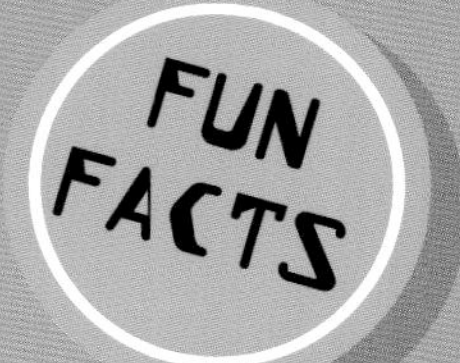


## Did You Know?

Most pirates wore the same clothes every day - and they didn't wash very often. Smelly!

There were a very few women pirates. They wore the same sorts of clothes as the men.

When attacking, the pirate **Blackbeard** put burning rope in his beard to look extrascary!

# Grub's Up!

After a few weeks at sea, a pirate's menu would be worse than a school lunch because the fresh food would have run out.

Pardon me!
Fart!
There's something stuck in my teeth!

**Dried beans** keep well, so bean stew was often on the menu. Pirates must have farted a lot!

To stop meat or vegetables from rotting, it had to be **pickled** or **salted**. Blech.

The **stores** were crawling with bugs.. so the food was, too. Crunchy cockroach, anyone?

FUN FACTS

Although most pirates liked to drink a tot of rum, **Black Bart** preferred a cup of tea.

Pirates loved to eat **turtles** because the flesh was soft, but it made their poop black and their pee green.

Three cheers for the captain!
Catch of the day!
WOW!

When freshwater ran out, pirates drank **rum**. Wine and brandy were for celebrating!

There were sometimes fresh meat and eggs - plus **fish**, of course, or **turtle**.

Hard cookies called **tack** would be full of weevils - tiny beetles.

In dock, pirates ate a mixed-up salad-stew of everything they had left - pickled stuff, vegetables, whatever - called **salmagundi**. The name comes from a French phrase that basically means "a weird mix of stuff."

**Buccaneers** were named after the French word for a barbecue cook - because that's what they did!

**Parrots** were kept as pets, but when the pirates got hungry enough, they soon became lunch.

# Party Like a Pirate!

Most pirates' idea of a good time at sea was being horrible to their victims... but when they landed on a safe island, they could stretch their sea legs, have a party, and go a bit wild!

Check out my moves!
PARTY

Pirates learned to walk in a wobbly way so they didn't fall over in stormy seas. They called it having "**sea legs.**" They'd still walk like this on land.

Pirates loved **music** and a good singsong. Each ship would have its own band of musicians to frighten enemies or cheer up the crew.

FUN FACTS

Pirates didn't really keep their **parrots** on their shoulders – they didn't want to be covered in parrot poop! They kept them in cages and taught them tricks.

Sailors crossing the **equator** for the first time would be dunked in barrels for fun.

Pirates pretended to have **trials.** One of them would be the judge and find new pirates guilty of being pirates!

**Card** and **dice** games were pirate favorites – they loved to gamble and would have bet their grannies if they could get away with it.

Some pirates enjoyed other things as well as games. **Captain William Dampler** liked nature – he was the first European to see a kangaroo.

Pirates drank chocolate like we drink coffee – the **South Sea** pirates drank about four cups every day!

# Pirate Booty

Pirates raided other ships for any stuff that was valuable. This could be all sorts of things. Some might surprise you!

**Sugar** was well worth stealing. In those days, it was very expensive and precious. It wasn't because pirates had a sweet tooth!

Pirates would often nab a **surgeon** from a raided ship to patch up their injuries!

Any **animals** that could be eaten - such as chickens and pigs - were very welcome on board.

Pirates would rob **jewelry** from ships' passengers.

Pirates got money from their captains to make up for losing **limbs** in battles. It must have cost them an arm and a leg!

**Captain Hornigold** once raided a ship and only took everyone's hats.

**Medicine** was really valuable to pirates as it kept them healthy on long voyages. Blackbeard once held the city of Charleston, South Carolina, for ransom for a box of medicines.
Pirates loved to steal fancy silk and calico fabrics in the Indian Ocean. They would wear the luxury cloths or sell them to governors in the American colonies.
This should help my toothache.
**Pieces of eight** were silver coins, stolen from Spanish ships. Gold **doubloons** were bigger Spanish coins.
One pirate captain, **Basil Hood**, was captured with a load of weird loot - some very sick cows.
The biggest-ever pirate haul was made by **Henry Every**. Each of his crew got about $1,500 - enough to make you a millionaire today!
WOW!

# Rotten Tricks

Pirates liked to avoid battles if they could. One way was to fool their victims into giving in instead of fighting. They had lots of tricks up their pirate sleeves!

Yikes!
Looking and sounding as scary as possible helped. The **band** would play, and the scary flag would be flown.
The best-known pirate flag is this one, the skull and crossbones, sometimes called the **Jolly Roger**.
There was also a **red skeleton** flag...
and a **sword and arm** flag. Yikes!
Pirates ahoy

They sometimes fooled their enemies by flying a **friendly flag** to pretend their ship was in trouble. When a ship full of treasure came to help, the pirates jumped on it!

If a crew had captured other ships, they could fly **pirate flags** from them, too, so that it looked like a whole fleet of pirates were attacking.

There are loads of them!
Fire!

FUN FACTS

Raids could be worthless. **Captain Calico Jack** once raided a ship and only got some tobacco and a few bags of peppers.

Pirates never attacked navy vessels because they thought they would lose.

WOW!

Raiders would pour nails, butter, and even peas onto a deck to make people fall over!

# Pirate Facts

Pirate captain **William Dampier** was one of the first Europeans to see and describe avocados, cashews, chopsticks, and barbecues!

Pirates didn't really make people **walk the plank**. That was a waste of time!

Anyone who broke a pirate ship's rules would be left behind on a **desert island**.

Pirate captains gave their ships **names** - scary ones, such as "Black Joke," "Flying Dragon," and "Tiger," or sweet ones, such as "Delight" and "Blessing"!

...and repeat after me.
Just chuck them to me!
HELP!
The Very Nice Ship (actually)
All aboard!